LeNNY LeMMON and the Invincible Rat

BEN DAVIS

illustrated by
JAMES LANCETT

nosy crow

Look out for:

LENNY LEMMON
and the
Trail of Crumbs

FOR ELODIE
B. D.

TO MY AMAZING WIFE MARTY
AND OUR FUTURE KIDDO WHO
WE ARE YET TO MEET.
J. L.

First published in the UK in 2023 by Nosy Crow Ltd
Wheat Wharf, 27a Shad Thames,
London, SE1 2XZ, UK

Nosy Crow Eireann Ltd
44 Orchard Grove, Kenmare,
Co Kerry, V93 FY22, Ireland

Nosy Crow and associated logos are trademarks and/or registered
trademarks of Nosy Crow Ltd.

Text copyright © Ben Davis, 2023
Cover and illustrations copyright © James Lancett, 2023

The right of Ben Davis and James Lancett to be identified
as the author and illustrator respectively of this work has been asserted
by them in accordance with the Copyright, Designs
and Patents Act 1988.

Printed and bound in Great Britain by Clays Ltd, Elcograf S.p.A.

Papers used by Nosy Crow are made from wood grown in sustainable forests.

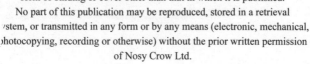

MIX
Paper from
responsible sources
FSC® C018072
www.fsc.org

1 2 3 4 5 6 7 8 9 10
www.nosycrow.com

OLDEN DAYS SCHOOL

"I wish you'd tell me what's in that box," says my best friend, Sam.

We're standing in the playground waiting for Ms Bottley to let us in. That's how we roll now we're in Year Five. None of that waiting-with-Mum nonsense any more.

They drop us off at the gate and that's that. It's a great system.

"Not a chance," I say, gripping it tight. "It's a surprise."

Sam stands back a little and fidgets with his fingers. He always does that when he's nervous. "But I thought I heard something moving in there," he says.

I tut and shake my head. "You and your

CRAZY IMAGINATION."

Sam is wearing a blue cloth cap, with a grey waistcoat buttoned all the way up to his neck. He doesn't always dress like that. The school asked us to come dressed up as kids from history. We're doing a whole day in

OLDEN DAYS SCHOOL.

That means old-fashioned lessons, no modern technology and the teachers act like teachers from hundreds of years ago. They reckon it's a good way to get us to learn about history or something, but that's not the important bit. You see, this isn't just

OLDEN DAYS
SCHOOL,

this is

OLDEN DAYS
WAR!

OK, maybe that's being a bit dramatic. It's more of a competition. But it is a very important competition. The Head, Mr Greenford, announced that whichever Year Five class does best at Olden Days School will win a **PRIZE**.

I glance across the playground at class 5A. They're lined up **PERFECTLY**, in total silence. Well, they would be. After all, they're

THE PERFECT CLASS.

They always get **PERFECT** grades, they always show **PERFECT** behaviour, and at the Christmas assembly they all sing like **PERFECT** angels. It's enough to make me want to throw up, to be **PERFECTLY** honest.

I can tell by the way they look down their noses at us in class 5B that they think they will **TROUNCE** us in this

OLDEN DAYS

competition, just like they **TROUNCE** us in sports, spelling, singing and everything else in the world. Well, not if I have anything to do with it. You see, I guarantee that no one else has brought in what I have. When Mr Greenford sees it, he will award us **FIRST PRIZE** straight away. To be honest, I don't know what the **PRIZE** is, but the **PRIZE** isn't

important. The main thing is that we beat 5A for the first time ever.

5A: 275

5B: 1 !!!

"You think my uniform is OK?" says Sam, running a hand down his waistcoat. "I've gone for authentic Victorian."

I would give him one of my trademark reassuring shoulder slaps, but I need both hands for the box. "Sam, you look straight out of *Mary Poppins*."

Sam gasps and clamps his hands over his chest like he's been shot. "But *Mary Poppins* is set in the Edwardian period!"

The classroom door opens and Ms Bottley stands there. She's wearing a white bonnet and petticoat and her face is **DEAD SERIOUS** and **STRICT**, even though she's not normally like that. This must be what teachers were like in the

OLDEN DAYS.

"5A CAN LINE UP IN AN ORDERLY FASHION, SO WHY CAN'T YOU? DO IT NOW!" She yells so loud it makes Kieran Roscoe squeak like a startled hamster. "IN ALPHABETICAL ORDER."

Now, hang on a second. No one seems to know whether she means alphabetical by first name or second name. My name is Lenny Lemmon so I'm in the middle no matter what, but Zoe Andrews is zipping up and down like

CRAZY.

"BY YOUR SURNAMES!" Ms Bottley booms. WOW. Why were teachers so LOUD in the

OLDEN DAYS?

I stick behind Amelia Kelly and eventually we sort ourselves out. I see Sam near the head of the queue, standing up so straight he looks like he's swallowed a rake.

Amelia, who is holding a tub of what looks to be sick, turns round and looks at my box. "What's in there?" she asks, all snooty like normal.

"None of your beeswax," I say, pulling it closer. "What's in yours?"

"It's gruel, like orphans used to eat. I made it myself," she says, then sticks her tongue out.

"KELLY! FACE THE FRONT!" Ms Bottley yells.

I can't help but snigger to myself. Amelia never normally gets told off. Maybe the

won't be so bad after all.

"You may now enter the classroom and

stand behind your desks," says Ms Bottley. "IN SILENCE!"

Inside, everything is different. For one thing, the tables are all gone. I'm usually on Red table, with Sam, Hugo, Parvati and Lydia. Now there are only little desks that seat two, and there are name tags on each one and OH GREAT, I HAVE TO SIT NEXT TO AMELIA.

"Oh no," she says.

I blow her a silent raspberry. I'm not exactly skipping for joy about it either.

It's only then I notice a WEIRD thing by Ms Bottley's desk. It's a huge black square on a wooden frame. At the top of it, in white writing, it says "FRIDAY".

"Hey, miss, what's that?" I ask.

"SILENCE!"

Ms Bottley shouts. "CHILDREN SHOULD BE SEEN AND NOT HEARD!"

That sounds WEIRD. I'd rather it be the other way round. Like, being invisible but still having a LOUD voice. I'd go up behind my brother while he's trying to do his stupid skateboard tricks and yell "BRANDON IS A STINKFACE" so loud he falls off.

Everyone is standing behind their chairs rather than just sitting down. Why? Why did

 OLDEN DAYS

people think up all these **WACKY** rules? It would have been bad enough living in a time with no Xbox without all this added stress.

"If you must know," says Ms Bottley, "this is a blackboard."

Makes sense. It's a board and it's black. It looks old too. Hey, if it helps us win the **PRIZE**, I'm fine with it.

"How can you not know that?" Amelia whispers at me through the side of her mouth. "You're so stupid."

Before I can reply, Ms Bottley **BARKS** at us to sit down. She's normally really nice, so this is **WEIRD**.

She picks up a tiny white stick and starts writing on the blackboard with it. It makes a

HORRIBLE SQUEAKING NOISE

that makes my teeth itch.

Amelia frowns at my box, which I've carefully placed on the table. "That stinks," she whispers.

"So do you," I reply.

She kicks me under the table and I cry out.

Ms Bottley spins round. "**WHAT IS THE MEANING OF THIS?**"

"Amelia kicked me!" I say.

"Did not!" she shoots back. The liar.

"One more

OUTBURST

from either of you and I will send you **BOTH** to the Headmaster's office," says Ms Bottley.

That's not a big deal to me. I'm always in there. And not because I'm naughty or anything. I'm always trying to do

THE RIGHT THING.

But

THE RIGHT THING

isn't always

THE RIGHT THING,

it turns out. Mum says it's because I'm

UNIQUE.

I look over at Amelia. She's gone all **PALE.**
If she got sent to Mr Greenford's office,

it would be a **HUGE DISGRACE**. Like the King being handcuffed and bundled off to jail.

"Now," Ms Bottley goes on, "I see you have all brought in some historical items. Bennett has a full costume. Very good."

Sam beams with pride. Or relief, probably.

"Kelly has brought in a pot of gruel." She points to a table at the back of the room where Amelia's tub of sick sits stewing. I think I'll be at the back of the queue for that, thanks very much.

"And I see Sharma has brought a book: *Wuthering Heights*. Good."

Wuthering Heights is a book? I thought it was this rubbish old song Mum always sings when she's in the car with the windows down. She sounds like a cat out in the rain, desperate to be let into the house.

Ms Bottley goes all around the class, complimenting everyone on their

OLDEN DAYS

stuff, but I see her eyes falling on my box every now and then. I bet she's saving it for last because she knows I've brought something really special. Something 5A

could only **DREAM** of. Plus, Amelia keeps staring at it and scooching away from me. She's such a snob.

"OK, Lemmon," Ms Bottley finally says. "What have you brought?"

I grin at her. I'm not sure if grinning had been invented in the

OLDEN DAYS

because everyone always looks dead miserable in **OLDEN** paintings and photos, but I decide to take my chances. "I'm glad you asked, Ms Bottley. Because I've brought

in something

VERY SPECIAL INDEED.

Something that is going to win us the **PRIZE**, no problem."

I see Sam staring at me from the other side of the room. He looks worried. Then again, he always looks worried.

"Stop shilly-shallying and show us then," says Ms Bottley.

Here we go. I open the flaps of the box, grip the metal handle and pull out the cage, placing it carefully down on the table. Amelia

SHRIEKS and runs across the room to the sink where we swill our paintbrushes.

"This is Ratty!" I say, pointing.

Inside the cage, the rat sits quietly, looking out at Ms Bottley. He seems to have calmed down a little since earlier on. I'm glad, because he's

BIG

and

SURPRISINGLY STRONG.

Ms Bottley takes a step closer. "Is that a REAL RAT?"

"Yeah!" I say. "I remembered that last week you told us there were loads of rats around in the

OLDEN DAYS,

so I thought this would be PERFECT!"

25

Ms Bottley looks like she's forgotten she's supposed to be an old-fashioned teacher as she peers through the bars at Ratty, who stands up on his hind legs and stares back at her.

"OK, Lenny. Well, it's certainly … different. Go and put it on the drawers over there," she says.

"But Parvati is allowed to keep her book!" I protest.

"Yes, but Parvati's book isn't scaring the

LIVING DAYLIGHTS

out of Amelia," Ms Bottley says back.

"It might," says Parvati. "There's a

GHOST

in it."

"Just..." Ms Bottley stands up straight and rubs her forehead. "Be quiet and put the cage on the drawers."

I exchange a look with Ratty, a bit like, "I'm sorry, mate," and take the cage over to the drawers. I put him in front of the books display board so at least he's got something to read.

When I get back to my seat, Sam is still staring at me, but Ms Bottley YELLS at everyone to face the front and his head whips round so fast, he looks like he's been attacked by an invisible ninja.

Everything's really boring after that, mainly Ms Bottley writing a load of nonsense on the board, which we copy down into our books. And Amelia STILL shields her work from me. What could I possibly be copying from her? And don't get me started about the sound chalk makes. It's

TRULY HORRIBLE

and makes my skin go **ALL SHIVERY.**

Ugh. How did

OLDEN DAYS

kids stand for this? Super-long days of boring school, before going home to a cold house with no TV and catching some horrible disease of the lungs and having to live in a metal tube for the rest of your life? No thanks.

"Now, you will be drawing geometric shapes," Ms Bottley booms. "You may go to your drawers if you need equipment."

Amelia puts her hand up. "What is it, Kelly?" says Ms Bottley.

"My drawer is next to the rat, miss."

Ms Bottley sighs wearily. "Lemmon, go and move the rat off the drawers so Kelly can fetch her things."

Normally, I'd be annoyed at having to get up and do stuff, but I want to check on Ratty, so I'm happy to make the five-step journey.

I pick up the cage. Huh. This might be a problem.

"Ms Bottley," I call out.

"WHAT HAVE I TOLD YOU, LEMMON?

DO NOT SPEAK WITHOUT RAISING YOUR HAND!" she yells back.

I raise my hand.

"What is it, Lemmon?"

"RATTY'S ESCAPED."

31

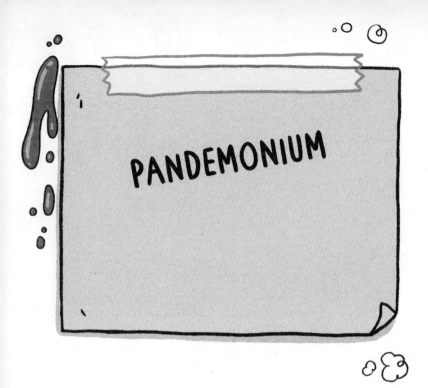

Pandemonium. That's a pretty big word. I've never really understood what it means. Until now. Amelia is standing on the table,

SCREAMING.

And she's not the only one. Sam is curled up in a ball on his chair. Ms Bottley is running around trying to calm everyone down. I hope Mr Greenford doesn't come in now because no one is acting

OLDEN DAYSEY.

"Relax, will you?" I shout over the noise. "It's only Ratty!"

But no one listens. Ms Bottley rifles through her drawer, pulls out a whistle and blows it long and LOUD until everyone is quiet.

"I need everyone to remain calm," she says. "We will not achieve anything by panicking. If a rat had got into an

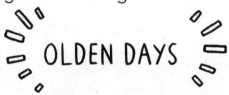
OLDEN DAYS

classroom, would they have panicked?"

No one says anything. All I can hear is Amelia gently snivelling next to me. I don't understand how Ratty got out. The cage door was closed. He must have broken it

open using his

INCREDIBLE STRENGTH.

"Everybody stay where you are, and Lenny and I will find his pet rat," she says.

I stick my hand up.

"What is it, Lenny?"

"He's not my pet rat."

Ms Bottley looks confused. "What do you mean?"

"Ratty's not my pet. I found him over the road from my house by the bins and put him in an old hamster cage."

Ms Bottley goes all **PALE** and has to sit on the edge of her desk. "So what you're saying is, you've brought a

WILD RAT

into school?"

"Yeah!" I say, not understanding why everyone's treating this like it's a **BIG DEAL**. "You wanted something from the

OLDEN DAYS!"

"She didn't mean disease-carrying rodents,

you imbecile!" Amelia shrieks.

"We're all gonna die!" Kieran Roscoe screams, and once again

PANDEMONIUM

reigns.

This is **RIDICULOUS**. If this is how they react to a rat on the loose, what would they do if there was, I don't know, a tiger?

Ms Bottley picks up the walkie-talkie she normally uses to contact the Head, but

then throws it down. "I can't believe I took the batteries out of this thing," she says. **"I'M NEVER DOING OLDEN DAYS SCHOOL AGAIN!"**

I see movement in the far corner of the room. It's Ratty!

"There he is!" I yell, pointing at him. This doesn't calm anyone down. In fact, it has the opposite effect. Everyone runs away, almost knocking Ms Bottley over. I pick up the cage and head over there. I tempted him in once and I can do it again. This time I don't have a big wodge of cheese, but I'll manage.

I see Ratty under the sink. He stops for

a second and looks at me as I slowly edge towards him with the cage door open.

"Here, Ratty, hop in for me, there's a good boy."

Ratty seems to think about it for a second, then scurries away behind the drawers. Maybe this won't be that easy after all.

"Stand back, Lenny." Ms Bottley comes over. "I can't have you putting your health at risk trying to catch a rat. Again."

Ms Bottley carefully pulls out the drawers one by one, including mine, but thankfully she's too busy worrying about Ratty to notice my comic, "*Mr Greenford Stinks of Wee and*

Cabbages". She stacks all of the drawers on top of each other, then crouches and peers into the darkness. She quietly picks up a magazine and rolls it up.

"Ms Bottley," I whisper. "It's a rat, not a spider."

She ignores me and leans further in. Where is he? Where could he possibly have got to? Then, suddenly:

WAAAAAAAAOOoWww!

Ratty leaps from the shadows and lands on Ms Bottley's Old-Timey hairdo. She

SCREAMS and FLAILS her arms around, sending Ratty skidding across the classroom floor.

43

Everyone scatters, desperate to get away, and in the crush I lose track of him.

"He went under your desk, Ms Bottley!" Henry Richards yells.

Ms Bottley, as red as a tomato with sunburn, stomps over, now armed with two magazines. I follow her for support. I get on my knees to look for Ratty but …

SPLOOOOOSH!

I jump to my feet just in time to see Ratty at the other end of the room, diving straight into the sick tub.

"Nooooo! My gruuuuueeell!" Amelia screams.

"Looks like he's enjoying it, at least," says Parvati.

By the time we reach the tub, Ratty has jumped out and is skittering across the room, leaving a trail of gruelly destruction.

The classroom is **LOUDER** than I've ever heard it, with **SCREAMING**, **SHOUTING** and **PANICKING**. Sam grabs me by the collar.

"**WHAT HAVE YOU DONE, LENNY?**" he yells. "**YOU HAVE RUINED OLDEN DAYS SCHOOL!**"

The shouting gets louder and louder, but then a noise cuts through it. It's a noise like I've never heard before; LOUD and PAINFUL. Everyone stops and turns towards where the noise is coming from.

I clamp my hands over my ears and look at Ms Bottley's desk. Standing there is a girl I've never seen before. She's wearing a Fleurwood Primary uniform but has her jumper sleeves rolled up, which is banned by Mr Greenford. One hand is planted on her hip while the other is extended outwards, her fingernails SCRATCHING down the blackboard.

When she finally stops making that brain-shredding noise, the room is completely silent. The girl steps forward and looks at all of us, her eyes narrowed.

"So you got a rat problem, huh?" she says. Her voice is strange. It's low and gargly. Plus, she sounds like she's from America. I've never met someone from America before. "Well, I'll catch it for ya, but it ain't gonna be easy."

"Um, excuse me?" says Ms Bottley. "Who are you?"

"This rat, swallow you whole," the girl goes on, ignoring Ms Bottley. "Little shakin', little tenderisin', down you go. And we gotta do it quick, that'll get

OLDEN DAYS SCHOOL

back on track. But it's not gonna be pleasant. I value my neck a lot more than three House Points, chief. I'll find him for three, but I'll catch him and kill him for ten. But you've gotta make up your minds. If you want to stay alive, then ante up. Ten House Points for me by myself. For that you get the head, the tail, the whole darn thing."

The room goes completely silent. I bet even Ratty, wherever he is, is staring at this girl. Ms Bottley looks confused for a couple more seconds, then clicks her fingers. "Wait, are you Jessica Conrad?"

"News travels fast," the girl says with a chuckle. "Call me Jess."

"But Mr Greenford told me you weren't due to start until next week," says Ms Bottley.

The girl, who I'm now pretty sure is Jess, shakes her head. "Old man gave you some faulty intel. Now, come on, you giving me the ten House Points or what?"

Ms Bottley shakes her head like she's trying

to dislodge water from her ears. "Sorry, we don't actually do House Points at this school. And anyway, I can't have you hunting and killing a rat. We'll have to do our outdoor learning while I sort out pest control."

Jess holds up her hands. "Your loss. By the time the boys in the truck arrive, this classroom will be nothing but RUBBLE."

Ms Bottley gets us all outside and up on to the school field, with a quick stop-off at the staff room to fetch her iPhone. Not very OLDEN DAYS.

"OK," she says, rubbing her forehead again. "Why don't you kids, I don't know, try and find some interesting leaves or something?"

I take a seat under the **BIG TREE**. My usual lunchtime routine is to hang upside down from one of the branches like a bat, but I know Ms Bottley wouldn't stand for it. Besides, I'm too annoyed that 5A are going to win

OLDEN DAYS SCHOOL.

I can see them now, all

PERFECTLY

filing out into the playground. All Ratty had to do was stay in his cage for a day but instead he escaped and RUINED EVERYTHING.

Who knew a rat could be so untrustworthy?

As I sit and ponder our next move, I think about Dad and wonder what he'd say. See, he's an inventor. Well, calling him that is a bit of a stretch. None of his inventions actually work. None of them. His self-walking shoes,

his talking toilet, his social media app just for old ladies (InstaGran). All of them end up blowing up. That includes the pest-control robot he made the other week. He told me it could hunt down all the rodents in any house and suck them up like a vacuum cleaner. The problem with that is that it couldn't tell the difference between mice and any other types of rodents, and let's just say our pet hamster Mr Snuggles hasn't been the same since.

Sam comes and crouches next to me. I can tell he's worried about getting green on his old-fashioned trousers.

"Lenny," he hisses at me. "Are you **CRAZY?**"

"I don't get you, Sam," I say. "Most of the time you're moaning at me for not taking school seriously enough and now, when I really do try to join in, try to win us all a PRIZE, you're still not happy."

Sam breathes heavily like he's just done a two-hundred-metre sprint in a suit of armour. "But … but … but…"

I sense a figure sitting down next to me. I turn round and see it's the new girl. Jess. There's a change in the atmosphere, like Darth Vader has just walked in. She stares off into the distance and rips up a handful of grass.

"Word on the street is you're the kid that unleashed the rat," she says, still looking at the horizon.

"Um, that's right," I say. "But it was an **ACCIDENT.**"

"You didn't 'ACCIDENTALLY' catch a **WILD RAT** from by the bins and bring it to school, Lenny," says Sam, doing the rabbit ears with his fingers and everything.

"Way I see it," says Jess, "you made the mess, you clean it up. But I can help."

"No," says Sam. "Ms Bottley is calling an exterminator. We just have to stay out here and wait until they've done their business."

Jess shakes her head. "These professional exterminators ain't nothing but a bunch of LILY-LIVERED CON ARTISTS. You'd have more luck sending in a baby lamb."

"How do you know?" says Sam, getting so annoyed that he WOBBLES on his heels and lands BUM-FIRST ON THE GRASS. "What makes you such an expert?"

Jess turns her head for the first time and fixes her eyes on Sam. She plucks a long piece of grass and clamps it between her teeth. "I come from the east coast of America. A place called Felicity Island. You might think it's a picture-postcard town

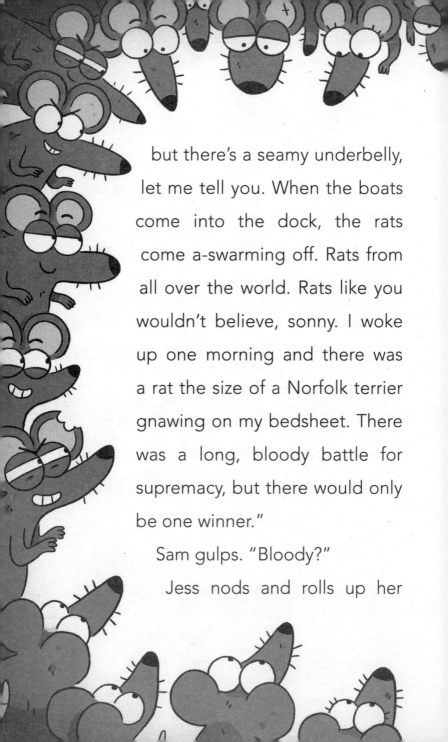

but there's a seamy underbelly, let me tell you. When the boats come into the dock, the rats come a-swarming off. Rats from all over the world. Rats like you wouldn't believe, sonny. I woke up one morning and there was a rat the size of a Norfolk terrier gnawing on my bedsheet. There was a long, bloody battle for supremacy, but there would only be one winner."

Sam gulps. "Bloody?"

Jess nods and rolls up her

right trouser leg. "See this scar?" She points at a long white line down her shin bone. "Got it that morning. A permanent reminder that rats have got to be taken out before they take you out."

"What do you **MEAN**, you can't come until tomorrow?" I hear Ms Bottley grumble down the phone.

Jess shakes her head. "The rat will be too well established by then. He'll have moved his whole family in. We need to act now."

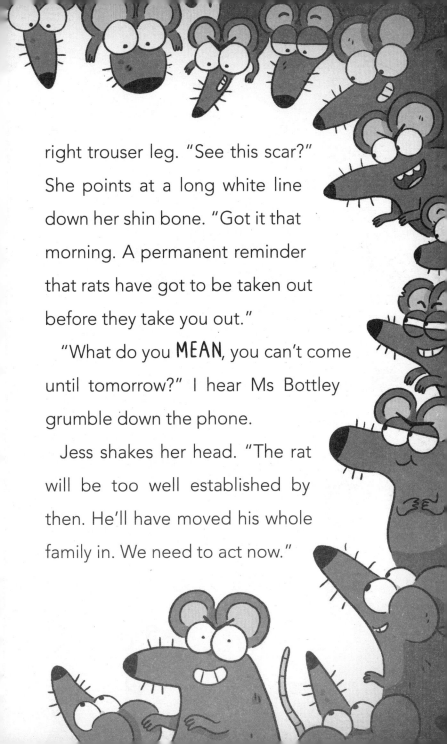

I can't believe what I'm hearing. "So you're saying we have to

SNEAK BACK IN

and get the rat?"

"Bingo," says Jess.

Sam goes to kneel, but then remembers grass stains and crouches on his haunches. "You can't be serious," he says. "There is no way we are doing that."

I ignore him and stand up. "No. Jess is right. I unleashed the rat and it's my job to get rid of it. Besides." I nod down the hill at

the playground, where 5A do

exercises in **PERFECT** time with each other. "There's still a chance to beat them."

Sam jumps up and stands in front of me, his arms wide like a goalkeeper. "I – I'll tell Ms Bottley."

He points over at her, standing with her back to us, still having a row with the poor rat exterminator.

"Will you?" I say. "Wouldn't that be against

a certain, oh I don't know,

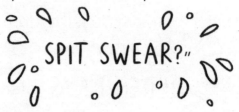

SPIT SWEAR?"

Sam **GROWLS** under his breath. He knows I've got him. Back when we were six, we gobbed into our hands and shook, vowing to always stick by each other through thick and thin, and never, **EVER** tell on each other. I was a

GENIUS

to think that up.

"Let's roll," says Jess, moving away.

I follow her, but Sam doesn't. I turn round.

"Are you coming or what?"

He skips back towards the rest of the class, then towards me. Forwards, then backwards. Then he groans and comes with me. I knew he would.

"Hey!" Amelia stands in front of us. She's still angry that Ratty gargled her gruel, I can tell. "Where do you think you're going?"

"We're going to speak to Mr Greenford," I say. "Ms Bottley sent us." I'm pretty good at making stuff up on the fly.

Amelia folds her arms. "You?" she says.

"Why is she sending you?"

Jess breezes past her towards the school. "Come on," she calls over her shoulder. "We don't have to answer her questions."

WOW. What a refreshing approach.

We find the door unlocked and walk inside: Jess first, then me, with Sam way behind. Jess stands in the middle of the room with her hands on her hips. "To catch a rat," she whispers, "you have to think like a rat."

I close my eyes and try to do as she says:

Mmm … bins. I love bins.

I'm snapped out of my dream by Sam screaming, "**THERE IT IS!**"

I follow the direction
of his **TREMBLING**
finger to see Ratty
squatting on the top
shelf of the bookcase,
furiously chowing down on
a thesaurus.

"That's **DISGUSTING**," says Sam.

"**REVOLTING**," says Jess.

"**REPELLENT!**" I yell.

Jess sprints across the room and jumps on
to the bookcase, which begins to topple. I
probably should have told her it isn't fixed
to the wall.

69

Jess dives for safety and tucks her head in for a perfect forward roll on to the carpet while Ratty scurries across the room and runs so fast he manages to get halfway up the wall.

"THAT THING IS NOT OF THIS EARTH!"
Sam shrieks.

Jess jumps to her feet and ZOOMS over
to the wall, where she picks up the net we
used when we were doing wildlife work at
the pond and Kieran Roscoe tripped over a
gnome and fell in and came out looking like
a swamp monster.

She bounds across the classroom and
SWOOPS on Ratty, bagging him in the net.
"Get me something heavy!" she yells.

I frantically search for anything that
would work and the first thing I see is this
HUGE ENCYCLOPAEDIA. I've never seen the

point of those when the Internet exists, but suddenly I'm all for them.

I press the encyclopaedia on top of the net. Ratty does not like this one bit and

THRASHES

with all the

FIERY FURY

of a tiny hairy dragon.

"Oh my goodness!" Sam cries.

Jess begins walking towards the door when –

BLLLAMM!

– Ratty tears through the net and lands on the floor with a **HEAVY THUD** before speeding across the floor and disappearing under Ms Bottley's desk.

I slowly walk over to Jess, spilled crayons crunching under my feet.

"You're gonna need a bigger net," I say.

ENDGAME

We try everything to catch Ratty, but every attempt just seems to make him quicker and angrier. He's like a rat version of the Hulk.

"Hang on!" Sam says, panting. "How did you catch the rat in the first place?"

"I lured him in with cheese," I reply.

Sam gasps, then finds his bag and pulls out his lunchbox. "I have cheese sandwiches in here!"

I smile to myself. Why didn't I think of that? Sam has cheese sandwiches every day. Good old predictable Sam.

"Great," says Jess. "Now we need something to trap it inside. Something strong."

I scan the room, then see the big wooden PE equipment box in the corner. It still has my "5B RULES!" graffiti on the bottom corner. I run over and empty all the balls, cones and rackets on to the floor. Jess comes over and taps the side with an approving nod. "Seems sturdy."

I take Sam's sandwich and pull out the slices of cheese, thankful he didn't have it grated.

I wave the buttery slices in both hands. "Here, Ratty! Some delicious cheese for you!"

Ratty scuttles out from under the desk and

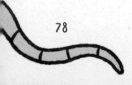

stands on his hind legs, his nose twitching, exactly like he did this morning by the bins.

I waggle my eyebrows at Sam and Jess, and whisper, "Prepare the box."

They pick it up and hold it behind me. Trying to ignore Sam's whimpering, I take a step closer, holding the cheese slices like they're hunks of gold.

"Come and get it!"

Ratty doesn't need any more encouragement and takes off across the room, straight at me. Super quick, I throw the cheese into the box and Ratty SMASHES in after it.

"SHUT THE LID!" I yell.

SCREAMING like a TERRIFIED PIG, Sam SLAMS his side shut, just as Jess does the same with hers.

"Let's get him out of here while he's still eating," says Jess.

Between the three of us, we drag the box outside on to the path by the playground, where 5A seem to be rehearsing some kind of play. Typical of them. They have their own PE box out and are too busy prancing around it to notice us.

"So what do we do now?" I ask.

"Are you serious?" says Jess. "It's obvious what we do."

I stare blankly so Jess shakes her head then draws her thumb across her throat.

"We can't kill Ratty," I say.

"Correct!" Sam shrieks. "That thing is more likely to kill us."

The box starts to

RATTLE ANGRILY.

"How does he still have energy?" says Sam. "After I eat a big meal I'm always tired!"

"Look, we'll just let him go," I say. "He won't bother us again."

"Who won't?"

Sam SCREAMS. So do I.

"Oh, hello, Ms Bottley," I say.

Ms Bottley's face is PALER than I've ever

seen it as she eyes the **WRITHING** box, then the open door to her classroom.

"OK, so we have good news and bad news," I say. "The good news is, Ratty has been contained. The bad news is—"

But I don't get chance to finish my sentence because Ms Bottley has walked past us and looked inside. When she turns and stares at us, she's gone so **PALE**, she looks like she's made of tracing paper.

"What happened?" she whispers, her bonnet falling down over her eyes.

Jess shrugs. "Big rat, big mess."

Ms Bottley runs a hand down her face.

"You three are going to Mr Greenford's office later."

"Noooooo!" Sam screams.

"But first, you're helping me tidy up this room." She jogs up the bank and calls everyone back inside.

"But, Ms Bottley! What about the rat?" I ask.

"We'll leave it in the box for now," she says. "At least we know it can't escape."

When Amelia sees the room, her eyes bug out of her head. "Well, this is just wonderful," she says. "First you ruin my gruel, then you ruin the classroom."

"Cool!" Henry Richards says, looking around at the carnage. "I wish it was

OLDEN DAYS SCHOOL

every day."

"The rat is taken care of," Ms Bottley yells. "Now, everyone pitch in and get the room back to normal."

As Ms Bottley wrestles with the overturned bookshelf, Jess shakes her head at me. "You're making a big mistake keeping that rat alive. A BIG MISTAKE."

THE PRODUCTION

The entire school is sitting in the hall, excited chattering bubbling everywhere. It goes silent, though, when Mr Greenford steps on to the stage. Next to me, Sam knots his cloth cap in his hands. He has never been sent to Mr Greenford's office and I can tell he's **TERRIFIED.**

We spent ages getting the room together but it looks almost back to normal now. Apart from the broken net and scratch marks and rat smell.

"Thank you, everyone," says Mr Greenford, holding up one of his hairy hands. "Now, as you may have noticed, Year Five is taking part in an

OLDEN DAYS SCHOOL DAY."

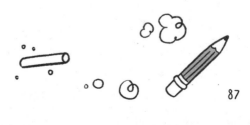

All the little kids turn round and stare at us over their shoulders. At least five of them are picking their noses at the same time.

"And I have said that whichever class puts in the best effort will win a **PRIZE**," Mr Greenford goes on. "So with that in mind, Class 5A have put together a wonderful assembly about the history of schools. Please give them a big round of applause."

I open my mouth and stick my finger in, making the "I'm gonna throw up" sign to Sam. That must have been what they were rehearsing in the playground. So typical of them to take it too far. I glance at Jess, but

her eyes are fixed straight ahead, while she runs a finger along the rat scar on her leg.

Three 5A kids in togas walk on stage. "Schools have existed since Ancient times," one of them says.

My heart sinks. I was so sure we'd beat them for once, but now it's obvious it's going to be them for the

FIFTY BILLIONTH TIME.

I stare at the wall and zone out as the production moves through history, complete with costume changes, songs and dances.

Mr Greenford sits in his usual chair at the front and to the side, tapping his foot to the beat while a kid called Lewis plays a flute solo.

I zone out again and only get my concentration back when I see a couple of kids lugging a wooden box on to the stage.

"PE has always been a hugely important part of school," some other kid says, but I can't take my eyes off that box. It isn't. Is it?

I lean forward and squint, hoping that will make me see better. They put the box down on the stage. Oh no. There it is. On the bottom corner, in my handwriting, it says "5B RULES!" It only looks like a smudge from here, but that's it. They must have got the boxes mixed up.

"Ms Bottley!" I whisper-yell, but she just gives me that "don't you dare embarrass me in front of the whole school" glare.

Sam jabs my leg. "What's the matter?"

I point at the stage. "That … that … that…" But my words won't come out.

"That what?" Sam hisses.

"Now we will show you PE equipment from throughout the ages."

They open the box.

Out comes Ratty.

PANDEMONIUM 2: THIS TIME IT'S PERSONAL

I thought what happened in the classroom was as **BAD** as it could get. Turns out I was

VERY WRONG.

When Ratty leaps out of the box, jumps off the stage and runs straight into the middle of the hall, it's like nothing I've ever seen. Everyone is

SCREAMING,

and I mean everyone: all the kids and all the teachers. Mr Greenford leaps across the room and starts climbing the bars like a terrified monkey.

Through the chaos, I catch a glimpse of Ms Bottley. Now she knows why I was trying to get her attention, but it's **TOO LATE**. The rat is out of the box.

We all jump to our feet and, through the hundreds of people running in **ALL DIRECTIONS**, I try and catch a glimpse of Ratty.

Jess stands next to me, her nose twitching like she's trying to sniff him out. "He's got to be around here somewhere."

I hear teachers trying to get their classes back into classrooms, but everyone is too busy running around and smacking into

each other. This is

TRUE PANDEMONIUM.

Still, at least 5A unleashed it this time.

"LOOK!" The **PIERCING SCREAM** of Amelia Kelly cuts through the noise. "**IT'S RUNNING INTO THE KITCHEN!**"

I snap my head round just in time to see Ratty's tail disappearing under the hatch, sending dinner ladies sprinting for the door like there's an oven fire.

Jess turns to Sam and me and grabs our arms. "Let's roll."

"Roll?" Sam yells back. "How will gymnastics help the situation?"

Jess shakes her head and sighs. "I mean, let's go get the rat."

"Absolutely not," says Sam. "I am already in enough **TROUBLE**. I am not getting in any more."

"But if we catch Ratty, we'll be

HEROES!"

I say. "As far as most people know, 5A brought the rat in, not us!"

Sam stamps his foot just like he used to when we were in Reception. "No! All this is your fault and I'm not going to be involved."

"What about the SPIT SWEAR?" I splutter.

Sam shakes his head. "The SPIT SWEAR works both ways, Lenny. If you really believed in it, you'd stay with me."

Oh. That's never happened before either.

The

SPIT SWEAR

was always my way of getting Sam on my side. Now it looks like he's figured a way out of it. I did not plan for this.

I look from Sam to Jess, and back to Sam. "I have to get Ratty," I say. "Like Jess said, this is my fault, so it's my job to put it right."

Sam shakes his head sadly. "Fine. Go and be with your new friend."

I'm confused. He said it's fine, but he said it in a way that made it sound like it

wasn't fine. Why doesn't he just say what he means? And why is he looking at me like that, all

SAD
and
ANGRY

at the same time? I'm doing what I think is best, and he's doing what he thinks is best. It's not like we're superglued together. Again.

Jess grabs my arm and **DRAGS** me through the **SEA OF SCREAMING** to the kitchen hatch, which she launches herself over like it's nothing.

On the other side, the kitchen is in full working mode, with bubbling pans and hot oven doors. There's a big chocolate cake on a trolley by the counter, all gooey and dark. It smells delicious, but I'm too busy to get hungry.

Jess picks up a big ladle. "If you bunch of softies had let me take care of that rat when I wanted to, none of this would be happening. Now, tool up. This ain't no Boy Scout picnic."

I look around for something of my own to grab, but only see a pair of oven mitts. Still, better than nothing, I suppose. I pull them on and try and imagine they are boxing gloves or gauntlets.

There's a HOT, NIBBLING FEELING at the back of my head and I think it's my brain trying to make me think about Sam, but I can't. I have to stay focused.

Jess crouches and stares at something on the floor. I kneel down and join her. She picks up a little brown nugget and gently squeezes it in her finger.

"This looks like fresh rat droppings," she says.

"EWWW! You're touching it with your hand!"

Jess ignores me and runs it through her fingers, before bringing it up to her nose

and sniffing.

"On closer inspection," she says, "it appears to be a Coco Pop."

Makes sense. We had Coco Pop squares for pud yesterday. They were delish.

We get to our feet and scan the kitchen for more clues of where Ratty has got to.

"Eyes on the prize," Jess whispers, pointing at the big island counter that splits the kitchen in two. "I take the left, you take the right."

I step round, going slowly, trying to listen out for noises over the hum of the ovens and the **SCREAMING** from the hall.

PpppPFffffsWWSShHhh!

A grey **FLASH** fizzes across the floor at the end of the island. Jess takes off after it and I follow, but when we get there, Ratty is nowhere to be

At the other end of the island, there goes another hairy bullet across the floor.

"This thing is fast," Jess breathes, patting the ladle in her palm.

PPPPPFFFFFSWWSSHHHH!

Ratty runs at us and knocks Jess off balance. She **SMASHES** into me, and I fall backwards. My arm hits something heavy.

KABLAMMMmM!

The pan full of bubbling sauce falls off the stove. I jump out of the way, but some of it splashes up my trouser legs. Most of it, though, coats the kitchen floor in pulsing, sticky gloops with steam rising off it.

It's a good thing I'm wearing this oven mitt or my arm would have been burned.

"When I get my hands on that rat..." Jess growls.

We head towards the direction we saw Ratty run in, but our shoes squelch in the sauce and we have to hold on to the counter to stop ourselves slipping over.

Walking that way sends us past the open hatch, but there's so much

PANDEMONIUM

in the hall that no one notices us. We scooch round to the other side of the island where the floor is drier.

"Come out, rat!" Jess yells.

THUNK.

I look up and see a grey tail on the end of the counter. By the time we get there, we find Ratty sitting in the middle of a huge Hawaiian pizza with his mouth full.

MUNCH!

"That's **DISGUSTING**," says Jess.

"I know," I say. "Pineapple on pizza."

Jess takes a swing at Ratty with the ladle but he jumps over it and skitters back down to the floor and along the island. We chase him round the corner but then my feet start **WILDLY SKIDDING** on the floor and, oh no, we're in the sauce, and Jess is **SKIDDING** too, and I try to hold on, but I can't reach and …

We both fall face-first into the sticky, warm red sauce.

I try and rub it off my face but more keeps falling down from my head.

Jess tries to stand up but slips over again. Then I do the same.

"There's only one thing for it," says Jess. "We're going to have to **DRAG** ourselves out."

So we use our arms to pull the rest of our bodies out of the sauce. Using a fridge door, I pull myself up, then help Jess to her feet. I try and rub myself down with my oven mitt, but that's just as **SODDEN WITH GOO** and there's no point.

PPPpPFFFFSWWSSHHHH!

Ratty ZOOMS along the floor at the other end of the island, but this time he WHIZZES through an open door, into a long, narrow pantry.

"Bad move, Ratty." Jess rubs her sauce-covered hands together. "We've got you cornered now."

"OK," I say. "So couldn't we just close the door and trap it in there?"

Jess shakes her head. "No. This ends now."

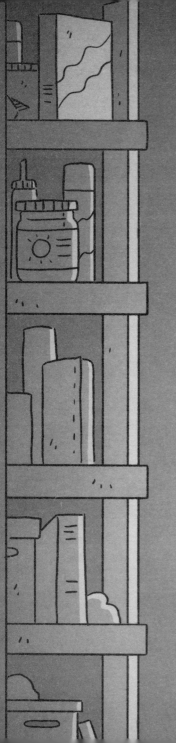

As we **SQUELCHILY** enter the pantry, I look around. It is lined on either side by shelves going all the way up to the ceiling. On these are every type of tinned food you can think of: beans, tomatoes, fruit, custard.

"Close the door behind you," says Jess. "We've got to trap it."

I do as she says, even though my stomach churns a little at the thought of being shut in such a small space with Ratty.

I remember seeing a movie my brother Brandon was watching when Mum and Dad were out and it had a rat that ate people in it. What if Ratty is like that? I wonder what I taste like anyway? I imagine bacon.

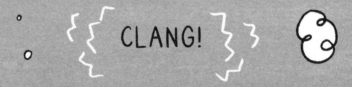

CLANG!

Jess whacks her ladle against a huge tin of peaches. "Come out and face us, you coward," she growls.

We stand still and listen. I grip my oven mitt extra tight, just in case.

SHHHHWWFFT!

Something sweeps along the top shelf to the left. Jess runs along, following the sound, and I go with her. She goes to jump up with her ladle when a huge canister tumbles off the shelf. I try to dive out of the way, but it's too late. We're hit.

CHECKMATE

Everything is white: the walls, the shelves, the floor. I rub at my eyes to try and clear them and keep blinking until I can make out Jess, who is also completely white.

"That rat tipped flour on us!" she growls.

Is that what it is? The sticky sauce makes it

cling to our skin. Wait a minute. Red sauce? Flour??? He really IS going to EAT us!

"But I don't want to be a bacon roll!" I cry.

"What are you talking about?" says Jess.

SNITTERSNITTERSNITTER!

A FLASH of grey snakes through all the white on the floor and disappears under a shelf.

"We've got you now, punk!" Jess throws herself to the ground and SMACKS her ladle around under the shelf, without making contact with anything.

"Where did he go?" she cries out.

I get down beside her and take a look. When my flour-covered eyes get used to the dark, I see a hole in the wall, big enough for a rat to get through.

Jess grunts and jumps back to her feet. "It escaped! Come on, let's get back out there."

I head for the door and pull the handle. Nothing happens. I try again. Nothing happens. Jess tuts, pushes past me and tries it herself. STUCK.

"Oh no," I say.

Jess sighs. "Outsmarted by a rat."

"What do we do now?" I ask, PANIC

beginning to flutter in my stomach.

Jess smacks the door with the ladle and her hand. "HEY, IS ANYONE THERE? LET US OUT!"

There's no answer. Of course there isn't. The dinner ladies ran away and no one else ever goes into the kitchen. This is

BAD.

This is

REALLY BAD.

"Oh no!" I yelp. "We're stuck! We're going to STARVE TO DEATH!"

Jess grabs me by the shoulders. "We're surrounded by food, GENIUS. Now, calm down. We're not going to get anywhere by pan—"

Jess stops talking and her eyes, like two pieces of coal in a snowman, get bigger.

"Pan?" I say.

But Jess doesn't talk. Instead, she SCREAMS. Really LOUD.

"AAAAARRRRGGGGH! GET IT AWAY! GET IT AWAY!"

She runs to the other end of the pantry and sits on the floor with her knees tucked under her chin. I turn round and look to see what she's so terrified of. Above the locked door, hanging by a tiny thread, is a spider. And not even a big one.

I go over and sit next to her, but something's bothering me. When she was SCREAMING, her voice sounded different. Much less low and gargly and American.

"Jess?" I say. "What happened to your voice just then?"

Her eyes dart around for a couple of seconds before she blinks hard and looks at me. "I suppose my secret's out," she says, her now completely different voice **WOBBLING** as she keeps her eyes fixed on the spider. "I knew it would come out eventually, but I didn't think it would be on my first day. Stupid spider."

"So you're not really from Felicity Island then?" I ask.

She shakes her head.

"And you never really fought a rat the size of a Norfolk terrier?"

She shakes her head again. "That scar on my leg is from when I fell off my scooter."

The spider starts to climb back up to the

ceiling, where it stays still, its legs tucked in.

"So why did you lie?" I ask.

Jess shrugs. "I didn't really have any friends at my old school. I thought I'd stand a better chance here if I became someone else."

My throat feels all

FUNNY,

like I want to cry. Poor Jess. I pat her floury shoulder. "I'll be your friend," I say.

She smiles a little. "Thank you." She shivers. "I don't mind rats, mice or anything like that. Spiders, though? **TERRIFIED.**"

We sit quietly for a while. Someone will find us eventually. They have to. And we can always eat bread rolls and cold beans until they get here.

"Aren't you scared of spiders?" Jess asks.

I shake my head. "I'm not really scared of any animals. Mum always says we shouldn't fear any of Mother Nature's creatures. I don't know if she'd still think that if a lion escaped from the zoo, though."

"So you could go over and pick up that spider?" Jess asks.

"Yes," I say. "Why? Do you want me to?"

"No!" Jess blurts. "I just don't know how

you could do it. They're so

HORRIBLE

and

WRIGGLY."

"My mum says all creatures are important. Like, if there were no spiders, we'd have billions of flies everywhere, flying into our mouths and pooping in our dinners," I say.

Jess frowns. "I've never thought about it like that."

"Everyone has a **SPECIAL SKILL**. Like me. Mr Greenford says I'm **NAUGHTY**,

but actually I'm

CREATIVE.

So Mum says, anyway. And you're really **BRAVE**. Except when it comes to spiders. Even Amelia Kelly has a **SPECIAL SKILL**. She's so **CLEVER**, she gives everyone else something to aim for."

"What about your friend?" Jess asks.

"Sam?" I say. "I don't know if he's my friend any more. But I know what his **SPECIAL**

SKILL is. You know your heart?" I tap my chest. "Most people have a heart about the size of a tennis ball. Not Sam. His is the size of a beach ball at least."

Jess gasps. "Does he have to take medicine for that?"

I laugh. "No, his heart's not really that big. But you'd think it was because he just cares so much. He cares about EVERYONE and EVERYTHING."

I sigh and my breath goes WOBBLY. I should have listened to him, shouldn't I?

CLUNK, CLUNK, CLUNK.

We both sit up straight. There's a noise outside. To begin with, I think it's Ratty, but it sounds too **BIG** for something so small.

"Help! We're stuck in here!"

After a second, the door creaks open. I ready myself for the telling-off from Mr Greenford, but it's not him.

"Sam!" I leap to my feet and run over to him, but he stumbles back.

"AAAARGH! GHOSTS!" he screams, scooping up a fish slice from the counter to protect himself.

I rub at my floury face to try and clear it. "Sam!" I cry. "We're not ghosts, it's me and Jess!"

Sam takes a long shaky breath and puts the fish slice back. I don't know what good that would be against ghosts anyway. It's not like you can flip them back to the other side.

"Why do you look like that?" he asks, squinting at us.

"The rat did it," Jess replies.

Sam looks confused, then looks even more confused. "Wait, did the rat change your voice too?"

"Long story," I say. "Thanks for letting us out anyway."

Sam bobs his head and scuffs the toe of his Victorian shoe on the ground. "I felt a bit bad about earlier. Sorry."

"No, I'm sorry," I say. "I should have listened to you, Sam."

I go to give him a hug but he steps back again. "Let's just shake hands, eh?" he says.

I take off my oven mitt and stick my hand out, then get a better idea. Through my flour-caked lips, I spit into my palm. Sam squirms a little, then does the same and we

SPIT SWEAR

all over again.

"Well, this is very touching, not to mention **DISGUSTING**, but don't we have a rat to catch?" says Jess.

I look at Sam. "What do you think?"

He draws his mouth into a pucker and nods. "Let's do it."

SHOWDOWN

There is still a **COMMOTION** in the hall when we get back into the main part of the kitchen, but it's starting to calm down a little.

"OK," says Jess. "No mercy."

We take a look around. **WOW**. Ratty has been busy. The sticky chocolate cake that sat on the trolley has exploded everywhere and a brown trail criss-crosses all over the floor. I follow it until it stops by the back wall where Ratty lies on his side, panting.

"It must have been the cake," Sam whispered. "When our dog ate chocolate, he had to go to the vet's and they made him throw it all up. Maybe chocolate makes rats sick too."

"Or maybe he's just resting," I whisper back.

I turn to Jess for her opinion, but she's already grabbed the trolley and is running at Ratty across the kitchen.

"I'M GOING TO ENJOY THIIIIIIIII—"

CRRRRRRRRACK!

Ratty scurries out of the way just before the trolley **SMASHES** into the wall.

I see him take off, squeezing through the gap in the door left by the fleeing dinner ladies. Sam runs over and closes it properly before Ratty can change his mind and come back in.

Jess stamps her foot. "It got away!" she grunts.

But I've noticed something behind her. Something on the wall.

"What is it?" says Jess, noticing me staring. "It's not another spider, is it?"

But I don't answer. Instead, I go over for a closer look.

There's a **BIG CRACK** in the wall, and

behind it, a long beam of wood. I chip away a little more from the wall and see another beam next to it.

"What is it?" says Sam.

I tap on the wood with my fingertip. "I'm not sure," I say. "But it looks like an old door."

DISCOVERY

Me, Sam and Jess are sitting in Mr Greenford's office. It's three days since we accidentally discovered a secret staircase that led to a **MYSTERIOUS CELLAR** under the school. It's all anyone in town is talking about. It's even been on the TV news.

Mr Greenford touches his fingertips together so his hands look like a little hairy tent.

"I must admit I'm unsure what to say to you three," he starts. "On one hand, you brought a rabid rat into school then caused

HUGE DAMAGE

trying to catch it."

I sense Sam breathing heavily next to me. He's been **TERRIFIED** about this **SHOWDOWN** all weekend.

"But on the other hand," Mr Greenford goes on, "you also discovered a previously unknown area of the school, complete with many

INCREDIBLY
VALUABLE
ARTEFACTS

from over TWO HUNDRED YEARS ago."

He runs a finger along an old leather-bound book on his desk. In the corner, there's a telescope, while a portrait of a scary woman stares back at us from the wall.

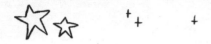

"Now, I've checked, and because these items were found on the property, they belong to the school," says Mr Greenford. He leans back in his chair and lets out a little chuckle. "Just think of all the things I can buy for the school with the money we're going to make: new books, better computers, a bus with working brakes. The sky's the limit."

I was thinking something more along the lines of a swimming pool, cinema and state-of-the-art gaming room, but I don't say anything.

"So, on balance, I have decided not to discipline you three."

Sam lets out a little squeak. He was **PETRIFIED** of his parents being called, because that would mean his

SCARY GRANNY

getting involved and coming down to the school. And he really didn't want that.

"Thank you, Mr Greenford," he says.

"But please," Mr Greenford goes on, "no more wild animals in school."

I struggle not to laugh when I remember him **SCREECHING** at the sight of Ratty. I glance over at Jess to see if she's thinking that too, but she's staring out of the window, her eyes distant. I can tell she's thinking about Ratty, still out there, gutted that she didn't get him.

"Can we go back to class now?" Sam asks.

Mr Greenford nods. "Yes. Best behaviour, OK?"

"Actually, Mr Greenford," I say, "there's one thing I wanted to ask you before we go."

He raises a bushy eyebrow. "What is it?"

"It's about the competition."

Mr Greenford lets out a little laugh. "I think the competition went out of the window

when **UTTER CHAOS** was unleashed, Lenny."

"I know," I say. "But all I want to know is, if you had to pick … I mean, if you really had to, would you say we won or 5A won?"

Mr Greenford shakes his head. "It doesn't matter. There is no winner."

"I know, I know," I say, holding up my hands. "But if you had to pick, like you had the choice between choosing a winner and dealing with another rat, what would you do?"

Mr Greenford **SHUDDERS** and swallows hard. "Well, I suppose I'd choose a winner."

I can sense Sam glaring at me, willing me

to shut up, but I can't. I'm too close.

"And who would you choose?" I say. "Bearing in mind that it was us who made a

MAJOR HISTORICAL DISCOVERY,

whereas all 5A did was half a rubbish play."

Mr Greenford sighs and runs his hand along a carved wooden box that was found in the secret cellar.

"I suppose I would choose 5B," he says.

I nod, not letting my joy show too much.

"That's all I wanted to know. Thank you, Mr Greenford."

As we leave the office and begin the walk back to Ms Bottley's classroom, I'm skipping with happiness.

"Why do you care so much about beating them anyway?" Jess asks.

"I've been wondering that for years," says Sam.

"Because we're a GREAT class," I say. "But people don't see it because 5A win everything." I jab a notice board in the hall with all of the gold stars under 5A. Their side of the board looks like a galaxy, while ours is more like, well, a few random stickers.

"But I can tell things are going to change," I say. "From now on, we are going to show 5A what we're really made of. No, strike that, we're going to show the WORLD what we're really made of."

"You know we didn't officially win the competition, don't you?" says Sam.

I wave him off. "Details, details. We all know what Mr Greenford really meant."

And with that, I throw open the classroom door. "Hey, everybody! Guess who beat 5A?!"

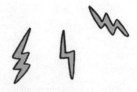